DON'T LOOK BACK

DON'T LOOK BACK

Emily Ann Davison

Illustrated by Sunnu Rebecca Choi

Collins

Places

Asphodel Fields – a place in the Underworld where you forget all your memories

Elysium – a happy place in the Underworld, where mortals who have lived good lives go

Mount Olympus – a mountain in Greece where ancient Greeks believed gods and goddesses lived

River Styx – the river that separates the land of the living from the Underworld

Taenarum – the town where the entrance to the Underworld is

Underworld – a place where dead souls go, believed to be underground

Characters

Apollo – god of light and music, and Orpheus's father

Cerberus – three-headed dog who guards the entrance and gates to the Underworld

Charon – ferryman who steers the boat and takes the souls of the dead across the River Styx to the Underworld

Demeter – goddess of the harvest, and Persephone's mother

Eurydice – a beautiful nymph (woodland spirit)

Hades – god and ruler of the Underworld

Hermes – messenger between mortals and gods, who also leads dead souls to the Underworld

Hymen – god of marriage

King Sisyphus – a wicked king whose punishment in the Underworld is to roll a heavy, giant rock up a hill, and as soon as it's about to reach the top, it rolls back down again

Orpheus – son of Apollo, and a talented lyre player, whose music enchants anyone who hears it

Persephone – goddess of agriculture, queen of the Underworld and Hades' wife

the three judges – Aeacus, Minos and Rhadamanthus; their role is to judge the dead in the Underworld

the three sisters (sometimes called the Fates or Moirai) – Clotho, Lachesis and Atropos; their important role is to make sure every being lives out their destiny

Prologue

My name's Orpheus. This is where I live, at the foot of Mount Olympus. At the top lives my father with the other gods. Father is of great importance. He's the god of music and light, and my mother is a muse, a goddess of poetry; she has the most enchanting singing voice. It's therefore no surprise that I have a musical gift too! Ever since I could speak, I've spent my days singing, just

like Mother. When I was a child, she taught me verses of different songs, and now I'm a young man, I still sing those same songs. They are etched into my heart.

My best friend Hermes often asks me to sing to him, when he's resting from his job. He's the messenger god, who sends messages between the gods and the people. He also guides souls of the dead from the land of the living down to the Underworld. We've been best friends for as long as I can remember. He's stood by me through everything, even my darkest days …

1 The lyre

I can't believe it! I stare down at the precious lyre in my hands. It has horsehair strings reaching down to the body made of tortoiseshell. I'm amazed that

it's so much heavier than I expected. I know it has a special place in Father's heart. It's been his treasured instrument for many years, a gift from Hermes. I've often longed to play it, but now the moment is here, I don't dare. What if I can't play the lyre well? Or what if I damage it? I never want to disappoint Father, so I pass it back to him.

"Orpheus," he says, "you have the most beautiful singing voice and musical talent. Now you are a young man, I want to gift to you this lyre."

"But Father, you love this lyre." I shake my head. "I couldn't possibly."

"Nonsense!" Father says. "You are my son. And I want you to have it. Here, please try."

The lyre looks much smaller in his hands. He handles the lyre carefully and passes it back to me.

I'm unsure at first. I've never played a lyre before. Suddenly, my stomach feels uneasy, and my mouth dry. I perch on a large rock, and fling my hand down on the strings, just like I've seen Father do. But my hands are sweaty, and I don't have a good grip on the lyre. It tumbles to the ground.

I jump up and gasp. Have I broken it?

On closer inspection, I see that I haven't. Thankfully!

"I'm sorry," I stutter. I can feel that my cheeks are glowing.

"You should try again," Father says warmly. His voice is soothing and rich. It always makes me feel like I'm warming by a flickering fire.

This time, when I touch the lyre, my fingers tingle. A warmth spreads through my hands, down my arms and throughout my body. I grip the lyre more firmly, and I strum the strings gently. The notes chime out. They're singing to my soul. I can't stop the smile from spreading across my face. I try again. It feels like I was born to play this lyre and I never want to stop. Father returns to his throne and home on top of Mount Olympus, with the widest grin on his face.

I decide to practise all day long, staying put on that very rock. I practise and practise and practise. As I sing along to the melody, joyful memories flash

into my mind. The lyre's music makes my heart swell. As the light begins to change, I realise the sun is setting, and I think I've finally mastered playing my lyre!

Under the bright moonlight, I strum the strings. My song fills the air. I spot a nightjar perching in a nearby tree. Its head is tilted, as if it's listening to me. As I carry on, the nightjar swoops down to my feet, and sways, mesmerised by the power of the melody. Then a second one arrives, and another, and another! A flock of nightjars are at my feet. And I play for them. I suspect that something extraordinary is happening. I decide to test out my theory tomorrow.

2 A powerful gift

As soon as the sky begins glowing burnt orange with the sunrise, I pick up the lyre and play.

I go outside and breathe in the smell of fresh blossom in the air. All the while, I carry on playing. A chestnut brown rabbit hops towards me, with others following him. The twittering of birds in the tree tops above grows silent. I look up, and they seem to be watching and listening. I make my way down to the river, through the long grasses. The rabbits and birds follow. I stop at a clearing, and step onto a tree trunk. Creatures gather around me in a circle, and as I play, they dance to the beat of my song. I feel a rush of something through my body I've never felt before. I'm at one with the music. The song echoes my feeling and becomes even more joyful.

Suddenly, something catches my eye. A brown fox is sneaking through the tall grass. I worry for the rabbits, but there's no need. The fox joins in our dance too. It feels as though the whole of nature has gathered around to be my audience. Even the rocks and trees seem to have edged closer to me. Impossible, I know!

Just as I thought, my playing has some strange power. Even more so than Father's playing, and that's saying something! I remember sitting on top of the mountain, listening to his music, surrounded by gods and mortals, like me. We'd sing along to his tune. But this is something else.

I rush home to tell Father all about it.

"I saw," he chuckles. "I've been watching. You enchanted all the nature in the wood!"

"It did feel that way," I murmur. "But that seemed like a dream."

"You have a gift, my son!" he says. "And that's of no surprise. Music is in your blood. It seems you were destined to be a great musician all along. I suspected as much."

It makes sense to me now. That's why he was adamant I should have the lyre!

"Tomorrow, I'll gather the gods, and you should play for them!" Father declares.

"Oh – " I shuffle my feet on the floor. Playing for nature is one thing, but for the gods?! That's something else entirely. "Maybe I should practise a bit more first."

"I understand, Orpheus," he says, placing his hand on my shoulder. "Why don't you perform for the mortals first? I'm sure you'll realise that you are more than ready to play for the gods."

"I'll ask Hermes to spread the word," I say.

"No need," says a voice behind me.

I startle and turn around to see Hermes behind us.

"I've been listening to your songs all day!" he beams. "I've never heard anybody make

music like you do. Tomorrow, I'll spread the word, and tomorrow evening, I'll bring you an audience like you can't imagine!"

I go to bed full of nervous excitement about tomorrow. I wake to the exact same feeling. The hours of the day drag on and on as I practise my playing, ready for my performance.

Evening is drawing in, and Hermes is true to his word. People travel from near and far to hear me play. Farmers, sailors, fishermen, merchants, wives and children. They all crowd round and listen. The farmers' animals arrive too! There are so many goats, donkeys, chickens and cows – too many to count! They stand as still as statues, mesmerised by the melody. Even the

wild beasts gather around. The wolves and bears seem tamed by the tune too.

Suddenly, a bearded farmer stands up. “Hey, I know you!” he shouts and points at a grey-haired man, who looks sheepish.

I stop playing and silence swirls around us all.

The sheepish man bows his head, avoiding eye contact with the farmer.

I feel uneasy and wonder what has upset the farmer.

“You stole a crate of barley from my farm,” cries the farmer. “I’d recognise you anywhere.”

“I’m sorry,” says the man, looking directly into the farmer’s eyes. “I admit it; it’s true. I’ll make it up to you.”

“You’d better!” The farmer spits out his words.

The man nods quickly and wipes a tear from his eye. He turns directly to me. “This music has moved me in ways I’d never have imagined. I vow to only do good from this moment on.”

A realisation suddenly dawns upon me. My music has more power than I'd realised. It can sway people to do good, and calm fiery situations. I smile at the man, feeling slightly embarrassed but also proud. I look to the farmer who nods at me to carry on playing. He seems content with the other man's reply.

I play on. A moment of calm fills the air, and I realise my purpose in life. To play the lyre for myself, and for others. Father was right: I have a gift! I will share it with the world!

As night settles in and the sky becomes scattered with stars, the crowd disperses and I decide I'll play for the gods tomorrow.

"Hermes!" I call.

"I'm here, Orpheus," Hermes chuckles, and suddenly pokes his head out from behind a tree. "I've been listening all this time to the music."

"Can you send a message to the gods? I'm going to perform for them at the foot of Mount Olympus tomorrow."

"Very well," says Hermes, and shoots off into the air.

I'm no longer nervous at the thought of playing for the gods! In fact, a buzz of excitement stirs within me.

3 Spellbound

It's a whole year after Father gifted me the lyre, and I'm an expert lyre player now. I know so many songs, and spend every day playing, from sunrise to sunset. Each month, I go to Mount Olympus and the gods come down from their thrones and I play for them ... well, nearly all the gods. Some are too busy doing their important jobs. I haven't played for Hades, the god of the Underworld, yet, and to tell you the truth, I'm thankful. The thought of that scares me. Hades hardly ever ventures out from the Underworld. He seems to prefer spending his time in the dark, amongst the dead and floating souls.

It's the anniversary of the first day that I played my lyre to an audience. I remember the warm feeling it gave me and I can't seem to remember a time before I had my lyre. I wander through a woodland and find a resting spot beneath an ash tree. I settle down and hum along to my lyre. My fingers dance over the strings. The chiming song reverberates inside the tortoiseshell, amplifying the sound. As usual, my playing attracts an audience. This time it's some tree nymphs. These spirits dance around the ash tree, giggling. They are beautiful, just like all nymphs are! Just then, something catches my attention in a nearby oak tree. Something keeps peeping out of the branches and ducking back within the canopy again. I stand, and stroll beneath the tree and pretend I haven't noticed. It happens again!

This time, I see what, or should I say who, is hiding. She's the most beautiful nymph I've ever seen. I glimpse a sight of her deep brown eyes and russet red curls, between the branches. I carry on strumming, meandering between the different trees. And this nymph follows me, ducking behind trees and hiding. Finally, she jumps out in front of me. Her green silk dress flutters in the breeze.

I'm speechless. This nymph is radiant. The sun seems to shine from her as she smiles at me. I smile back. I'm spellbound by her. She's the first to speak.

"Orpheus," she whispers. "They told me your music was captivating and truly it is."

"*You* are captivating," I say, and then I wish I could take back my words. Even though I do mean them. My cheeks warm with embarrassment.

"I'm Eurydice," she giggles. "Will you – " and she gestures to my lyre. "Will you play for me?"

"Of course!" I say. I'm much more confident playing, than I am speaking to her.

The light begins to dim, and I suddenly realise I've been playing to Eurydice for countless hours.

"I should go," I say.

"Will you come back tomorrow?" Eurydice asks.

How can I say no? "Gladly," I answer.

And that's how I meet the love of my life.

Each day Eurydice and I spend together is better than the last.

Today, the sun is beaming down upon us

and we're about to have a delicious picnic with goat's cheese and fresh juicy fruit.

"Before we enjoy this," I say, "I have something I want to ask you."

Eurydice's deep brown eyes meet my own.

I clear my throat and don't hesitate. "Will you marry me?"

She leaps into my arms. "Yes! Yes! A thousand times, yes!" she cries.

"We need to ask for Father's blessing," I say. "But I don't think that will be a problem!"

After we say goodbye to each other, I hurry home to ask Father.

"I'm so happy for you both," he says. "I'll ask Hermes to spread the word and send a message to all the guests! It will be the most jubilant day of the whole year. We'll have a feast like no other, and I'll ensure the sun is shining down on you both!"

I'm so happy that Father has given his blessing. I can't wait to spend the rest of my days with wonderful Eurydice!

4 The wedding

Today is the day! Since the day I met Eurydice, we've been inseparable, always in each other's shadow. I'm so excited to be marrying her today. The temple looks bigger than I imagined. The tall columns tower over me, and suddenly, my throat feels dry and my stomach uneasy.

I walk past the columns, and see Hymen, the god of marriage, waiting at the far end of the temple. With one hand, he adjusts his saffron robes. He looks a little anxious. The torch he holds flickers as if to greet me. The temple is decorated with candles and lamps; the warm light from them echoes my feeling for Eurydice. As soon as I enter, the guests nod and murmur, and wish me luck. The nymphs giggle as I pass. Before long,

Eurydice, my bride, arrives and a hush falls over the temple. I thought I'd be nervous, but I'm not. The anticipation I felt before subsides. Eurydice is even more beautiful today than the first day I laid eyes on her, and that's saying something.

We say our vows to each other, never breaking eye contact throughout, and then the moment comes.

"I now pronounce you husband and wife!" declares Hymen, and the temple erupts into cheers and applause.

Now it's time to share a feast with our guests. It's a grand feast, with olives, figs, cheese, fish and meat. I think some of our guests have never had meat before. I hear some ask what type it is.

"Deer? Those hunters must be talented to catch them!"

"It's so rich and delicious."

"Not for me, I'm afraid."

All of a sudden, Hymen calls out a toast for us. "Everyone ensure your cups are full. I'd like to make a toast," he begins, but as he does, his raised torch sputters and spits. A blast of cold wind rushes through the air. Dark smoke drifts over the feast. The fumes cause us all to splutter and choke. My eyes sting and start to water.

I hear murmurs amongst the guests, as they escape from the smoky feast.

"This is not a good sign for the marriage!"

"I agree. A terrible omen of what's to come."

I whisper into Eurydice's ear, "Don't listen to

them. This is the best day of my life, and the start of our lives together!"

"And mine," she whispers back. "A little bit of smoke can't deny us our happiness together."

We find ourselves alone; all the guests have departed. They should have guided us to the home we'll share together. They should have showered us with nuts and figs. They should have sung a marriage hymn to us; I had my lyre with me ready! But we only have each other left, to walk the path together towards our new home. I don't

mind in the slightest. It's been a long, tiring day. The ceremony in the temple feels like it was years ago, and I'm glad it's just the two of us. I take Eurydice's hand in mine and squeeze it gently.

"Before we go home, will you play for me?" she asks.

I nod, and we settle under an ash tree. I think it's the very one where we first met! I play to her the same song I played that very first time. She leans her head onto my shoulder, and I feel the happiest I've ever felt. If I could pause time right now and stay in this moment forever, I'd be happy. But I also can't wait to see what tomorrow will bring. Our first day together as husband and wife! I'm so glad we found each other; I'd be lost without Eurydice now.

5 The first day

It's our first day as husband and wife! The sweet smell of blossom wafts through the window, as we enjoy our barley porridge and fresh juicy grapes. I can't take my eyes off Eurydice. She smiles sweetly at me, and I grin back at her.

"Let's go for a walk before it becomes too hot," says Eurydice.

I grab my lyre, and she takes my hand and leads me out of the door. The air is already shimmering in the heat, as the sun beats down. We follow the meandering path, but the day is already warming up.

"We should shelter in the shade for a bit," I say, brushing the sweat from my forehead.

Eurydice nods and we stray from the path. The grass rustles underfoot as we make our way to an orchard.

"Here looks good." I point to the shade of an olive tree.

We sit there for some time until Eurydice shakes her head. "I can't bear how hot it is!" she moans. "I'm going to go to the stream to cool down."

"I'll wait here for you," I say.

I listen to her humming to herself, as she dances down towards the flowing stream. My heart skips in time with her steps. When I can't hear her any more, I pick up my lyre and play some music while I wait. Soon, I'm no longer alone.

At first a small field mouse scampers towards me, followed by a family of rabbits. A small gathering is at my feet. I laze back on the tree trunk and shut my eyes as I play. This is such a wonderful life to have. A life full of music and love. There's nothing better! As I play, I hear something in the distance that grabs my attention, or at least I think I do. Was that Eurydice's soft voice? I'm sure I hear my name. I stop and listen closely. But all I can hear is a faint hum. I look into the distance to try to spot her. The air is hazy and I can just make out a swarm of bees. I shake my head to myself. Her voice was just my imagination! The heat sometimes plays tricks with your mind. The bees buzz away and I continue my strumming.

As I carry on strumming, deer and foxes join the crowd of animals too. Even the trees seem to edge closer to hear my song better. I play to all

the nature around me. Even a snake slithers to join the audience.

Suddenly, I notice the clouds overhead. My stomach rumbles and I realise breakfast was quite some time ago. My mouth is dry too, and I need to drink. However, I dare not move from the spot. I promised Eurydice I'd wait for her here. What if she comes back, while I'm off searching for fallen fruit in the orchard?

The sun is beginning to dip in the sky, and

still there's no sign of Eurydice. A cloud breaks and rain begins to trickle down. One by one, the animals leave me with my song. The beat of the song slows down, and the notes clash with each other as I play. The wind howls over the lyre. I'm all alone, and I feel uneasy. Eurydice should be back by now. I don't know how long I've been waiting for her to return, but it's definitely been hours. Perhaps she thought we were meeting back at our home? I should go back home and see.

6 A search party

I weave in and out of the dripping trees, back to the path, and make my way home.

As soon as I see it, I feel relieved. I realise how uneasy I was and feel every muscle in my body relax. Of course, she must be there, inside, waiting for me! I rush inside and I call out to her.

"Eurydice? Oh, Eurydice, are you here?"

I hear a voice reply from the kitchen and I rush to it.

"I thought she was with you," says our cook, poking her head out of the kitchen.

"She's not here?" I say, breathlessly.

"I'm afraid not," says the cook.

"Oh – " I pause. I look out of the window. "I'll search outside. It's still light enough to see." I bite my lip, and mutter half to myself, and half to our cook, "She should be back by now."

"I can help," says the cook.

"Thank you!" I say. "I would ask Father to help, but he's away on his chariot."

"Between us both, we'll find her, I'm sure," the cook replies.

We split up and take different routes. I trace back the way we went.

“Eurydice!” I call. “Eurydice?”

But silence is the reply. My stomach is in knots.

“Eurydice!” I cry, even louder this time. “Eurydice! Eurydice!”

I listen for a reply, but my voice isn’t carrying over the wind. I’ve forgotten that I still have my lyre, so I try strumming it, thinking that will surely grab her attention. But the wind growls, and the chiming strings are drowned out.

I zig-zag through the long grass, trying to think which way she would have taken. I think I hear the stream rushing in the distance, but then there’s a flash above me. A thundercloud crashes overhead, and the sky rumbles. There’s little light in the sky now. How will Eurydice find her way home in the dark?

I refuse to give up, when suddenly the cook appears.

“I haven’t seen her,” she says, between breaths. “And it’s getting too dark to look now.” She grabs my arm. “You need to return home, otherwise you’ll get lost too.”

I throw her arm off me and shake my head.

"Orpheus!" she cries. "Listen … Eurydice is probably already home. She could be there waiting for you."

I hope so much that she's right. I imagine what Eurydice will say. *"Oh, Orpheus, there was no need to worry! How sweet of you to go out searching."*

I hope that this will be the greeting I get. I hurry home and race through the door, but the house is empty and dark and silent.

"Did you ask the other nymphs?" says the cook. "Maybe they saw her as she went down to the stream?"

"That doesn't explain why she isn't back though," I say. "But I can ask them in the morning, once it's light." I try to sound hopeful, but my insides are churning.

I wish to all the stars in the sky that the cook's right, and wish for her safe return. At the moment, there's nothing else I can do, but hope and wait.

7 A dreadful discovery

I sit all night waiting for the sun to rise so I can resume my search. I haven't slept at all. How could I?

Every inch of my body tells me that something is wrong. Eurydice has still not returned to me.

I can't go out and search yet. I feel helpless. There's only one thing I can do. I rush to our courtyard and look up to the stars. I wish upon them again.

"I wish for Eurydice to be safe and return home. Please guide Eurydice home!"

I stay there wishing over and over until the sun finally rises. I get back onto my feet and grab my lyre. It's time to go and search for Eurydice again.

Things look different this morning though. The path down to the stream seems longer and the trees' shadows stretch further than normal. My legs feel heavy. I step off the path, towards the stream. I can hear it rushing not far ahead. As I step through the long grasses, I spot something. A hand reaching out towards me through the strands of grass. As I step closer, I see red curls. There's no mistaking it! Eurydice! She's fallen asleep in the grass.

"Eurydice!" I cry. "Eurydice, wake up! It's time to go home."

She doesn't stir. I tap her gently and recoil my hand in shock. She's icy cold.

"Eurydice?" I whisper. I dare not think it. I know it's true though.

"Please wake up, Eurydice!" I brush a curl out of her face.

I grab her by the shoulders and shake her.

"Eurydice!"

I bring her close to me and hug her tightly. I can't believe it. My Eurydice. Dead.

I carry her back to our home. Her body is limp in my arms, and I notice something on her ankle. A puncture wound. Right there and then, I guess what happened. A venomous snakebite! My poor Eurydice. She was the gentlest spirit and would never hurt a soul, yet a snake took hers from me.

As I make my way back home, Hermes hurries towards me.

"I was coming to find you," he pants. "I wanted to tell you, but I see you've found her."

"What do you mean?" I say, stifling back sobs.

"I came across her a few moments ago," Hermes says.

I don't reply. I feel empty inside.

"We need to have a funeral for her, so I can escort her soul to the Underworld," Hermes begins saying, but it's too soon for me even to think of that.

"Later," I say. "I need to be alone right now."

Hermes seems to understand, as he leaves promptly.

8 Saying goodbye

The time has come to say goodbye to Eurydice and have her funeral. Hermes has arranged it for me. He's placed a coin gently into her mouth, otherwise the ferryman won't let her soul cross the River Styx and pass to the Underworld.

Just before dawn, we have a funeral procession to take her to the cemetery. All the nymphs from the woodland are there, along with many of the people who have heard me play. I don't really notice them though. I know they are there, but all my thoughts are blurred. I can only think about Eurydice, and how she's no longer here. With Hermes and Father at my side, we bury her. Then Hermes gives me a knowing look, and I realise it's time. It's time for him to escort her soul to the Underworld.

He flies off, with nothing more than a nod.

Back home, I drift through the empty rooms. I see my lyre resting against the wall. Anger bubbles up and boils out of me. I grab it and throw it onto the hard ground. I hear a thwang and turn to see two strings broken.

"For the rest of my days, I'll never play music again," I declare. Without my sweet Eurydice, there is no music in my heart. I collapse into a heap of sobs. My heart is shattered.

I keep my word. I don't pick up my lyre again. I don't even glance at it. I find myself wandering into the woodland towards the very tree where we first met. Silence surrounds my every step. The woodland has fallen silent too. A mouse scuttles to my feet and nudges my foot with his nose. I shoo it away. I want to be alone.

As I sit on the damp ground, leaning against the rough bark, anger seethes beneath the surface again. It's not fair this has happened. I hear rustling to the side of me, and a nymph with blonde hair which reaches the floor appears from behind a tree.

"We can't believe she's gone," she says. "We miss Eurydice so much. Please sing for me, to cheer me up."

I shake my head. "There's no song in my soul without Eurydice," I say, and I turn my back on her and walk away.

A trail of animals follows behind me. Are they waiting for me to play to them?

"Go away!" I shout. "My lyre is broken, and I'll never sing or play again!"

A dark rage fumes inside my heart. The animals scurry away, leaving me alone. I find myself aimlessly wandering. I walk day and night. I walk under the beating hot sun and through raging thunderstorms. I keep going until I kick something hard on the ground. It's a broken bowl, and I realise where I am. I'm outside the temple where Eurydice and I were married. This bowl had fallen when the guests ran from the smoke. They said it was an omen, and they were right! If only I'd listened, maybe I could have stopped Eurydice from leaving my side. Maybe we should have been more careful? I stare at the jagged crack on the bowl. It's broken, like my heart.

Inside the temple, it looks so different from before. There are no warm flames flickering to welcome me, only dark shadows. I sit at the altar for hours, before I go back outside. I don't want to go home, to an empty house. I don't know where to go now. I feel so lost. I'm sitting outside the temple, my head in my hands, tears streaming down my face, when I feel a heavy hand land on my shoulder. It's Father.

"Orpheus, my son," he says, "I can't bear to

see you so distraught. It fills me with sorrow to see you like this."

"Then find a way to return Eurydice to me!" I shout and fling his hand off my shoulder.

"Only one god has the power to do that. You know that! Hades is the god of the Underworld and he's the only one who can return somebody."

"Then go and tell him to!" I spit my words out. I know I sound like a spoilt child, but it's not fair that Eurydice was taken from me and we never got to spend even one day together as a married couple!

"Hades doesn't take orders from me," says Father. "I can't make him do that. However, I have an idea. There could be a way to return her to you. Go into the Underworld and ask Hades to return Eurydice to you, yourself."

I shake my head. "That's impossible! If he won't listen to you, why would he listen to me?"

"I think you know the answer," says Father, cryptically.

Wiping my eyes, I whisper, "I don't. Why would Hades do that for me, and not you?"

"You can persuade him with your music. Play for him! Your music can sway anyone. I'm sure that even Hades won't be able to resist your song."

"I can't," I sob. "The lyre's broken."

Father holds out his hand and in his palm are strings. "Then fix it," he says.

I think about it for a moment. The journey would be perilous.

"How would I even get there?" I ask. "Getting into the Underworld is near impossible. How will I even find the entrance?"

"Hermes can take you. He knows the way better than anyone," says Father.

I nod. The idea seems preposterous, and to confront Hades wouldn't be easy, and to persuade him surely impossible. But what do I have to lose? I've already lost everything. My love. My reason for being. If there's even the slightest chance of success, the risky voyage to the Underworld is going to be worth it.

I go to the cemetery, with my lyre. I sit by the place where we buried Eurydice and fix my lyre with the new strings. My hands tremble as I play for the first time in ages. I sing to her about what I am going to do, that I'm going to get her back, no matter what.

9 The perilous journey begins

Living people don't go to the Underworld. I've heard about how to reach it, but I'd never be able to find my way. Thankfully, Hermes has agreed to take me.

"We need to go," I say to Hermes the next day, picking up my lyre.

"I know," says Hermes, taking a bite into some barley bread. "But let me at least finish my breakfast first."

I sit and stare at him until finally he stands up and brushes the crumbs off himself.

"I'm ready. Orpheus, listen, I can only get you as far as the River Styx, and then you're on your own."

"I know," I say. "I need to do this on my own anyway."

"I should warn you, the ferryman only lets the dead pass the river." Hermes sighs and frowns at me. "I'm sorry to say, I can't see this working. He'll never take you."

"I will find a way!" I say boldly. "The only way to cross the river is in Charon's boat, so I have to make sure that he doesn't turn me away."

Deep in my heart, I know there's a slim chance of this working, but I have to try. The river connects where the mortals live to the Underworld, and it's my only way to reach Hades.

We make our way to the town of Taenarum, where the entrance to the Underworld is.

"We'll go around the edge," Hermes mutters. "The townspeople will wonder why I'm escorting somebody living. They've only seen me lead the dead here."

I think of him leading Eurydice down here. I want to ask if she was afraid. But I'm afraid of his answer, so I say nothing.

"This way," he says, gesturing to a shadowy, gloomy woodland. He leads me through a well-trodden path. The woodland smells damp and earthy. Everywhere is eerily quiet, sending shivers down my spine. Finally, we reach a dark cave. I've heard many things about this cave. It's the entrance to the Underworld. To me, it looks like any other cave. You'd never guess what lay at the end of it.

"Follow me," whispers Hermes. His whispers echo down the long chamber.

I take a deep breath, and stay close behind him, following him as we venture down the sloping cave. It's wet underfoot, and each step sends echoes of splashes through the cave. The ground is slippery, and I nearly lose my footing on numerous occasions. The tunnels twist left and right like a coiled snake. It's even darker now, and I trust that Hermes knows the way. I know he's led many souls to the river, so I'm sure he does. My heart feels heavy, but with each step, I feel a bit bolder and braver. I'm doing this for my Eurydice. When I return, she'll be with me. I vow to myself that I won't leave the Underworld without her.

"We're here," says Hermes.

"I can't see a river or the ferryman," I say, squinting. It just looks like a barren land.

"Just around the corner," Hermes says, hovering ahead.

I wrap my arms around myself. The air

has become chillier. I sense that we're not alone. Mist swirls around me like a shroud.

"It's the souls who walk the riverbank," says Hermes. "Their relatives didn't provide payment to Charon, so he wouldn't let them cross the river."

I feel pity for these souls. They are forever destined to walk the riverbank. I quicken my pace, worried they'll whisper horrors to me, or touch me.

"They can't hurt you," says Hermes, sensing my trepidation.

"I know," I say. "But I still don't want to hang around here."

As we walk on, neither of us speak. The whispers around us rise and fall like a tide. They grow louder until it's all I can hear. They moan and cry and holler. I try to ignore the biting cold. I try to ignore the mist of lost souls. I try my very best, but I can't go on any more. I crouch and cover my ears. I can't remember why I'm here. I don't want to be here any more. I want to turn back. I want to go home. Back where the sun is beating down. Back to the warmth.

Hermes drags me to my feet and faces me. "We're nearly there, Orpheus! Don't give up now."

Suddenly, I remember why I'm here. Of course I won't give up! How could I?! I snap out of it, and march onwards. I strum my lyre to drown out the cries of the spirits around me and sing a song about love taken too soon.

"All it took was a snake, to snatch away my heart,
We were joined together, and then ripped straight apart."

The cries and whispers around me fall silent. The mist parts so we can pass through easily. Up ahead, I can see it! I can see the river!

10 Payment for the ferryman

The River Styx isn't like any other river I've seen. The water isn't clear like the rivers back home. It doesn't have luscious reeds floating along the rippling waters. It's as inky black as oil and as thick as treacle. A misty soul looks forlorn on our side of the river. It wanders towards the huge mist that envelops us.

“I dropped off that poor soul earlier,” whispers Hermes. “She didn’t have a coin.”

The soul can no longer be made out. It seems to have become a part of the whole mist now. I look back to the river. The ferryman is hunched on his boat, pushing his pole along the riverbed as he steers. Three misty figures sit opposite him.

The boat slowly crosses to the other side, where I can just make out a shadowy land. It has to be the Underworld. I'm so close now!

We wait for the ferryman to return. I need to seem confident to convince Charon to let me on his boat. I remember what Father said to me when I was little. Act brave and courageous and you'll trick the world into thinking you are. So, I lift my head high and stick my chest out. Oh, I wish Father were here now. He could shine a light into the darkness of this place. But I need to do this alone. Apollo has no place in the Underworld.

When Charon returns, I clench my fists, so he can't see my hands trembling. The ferryman looks as tired as his rusty red boat does. His clothes are tattered and his hair as grey as the cave we passed through.

"Another soul for me?" says Charon, in a gravelly voice. "Does he have a coin, Hermes?"

"No, Charon. He doesn't," says Hermes.

Maybe we should have brought one, I think.

"Then he can't gain passage in my boat! This soul

will wander the riverbank forever!" growls Charon.

"I can't do any more for you," says Hermes, tapping my back. "And I have to get back. There are more souls that need escorting here. I wish you the best of luck."

I nod to him. "Thank you, Hermes. May we meet again with Eurydice at my side."

I watch Hermes depart and then I take a step closer to Charon, ready to state my case.

"But wait, what is this?" Charon squints at me and strokes his beard. "Come here!"

I obey and stand right before him. I'm so close that I can feel his breath on my face, and he must be able to feel mine on his.

"Why, you're not even dead! Turn around and go back to where you came from!" He shakes his fist at me.

"No." I take a deep breath and declare, "Let me cross, Charon. I have business with Hades." I sound braver than I feel.

Charon chortles at this. "Business with Hades! Hades will have no interest in you, unless you're dead. Turn back!"

"I can't. I need to cross this river."

Charon shakes his head. "Everyone must make this trip, but it isn't your time yet," he says gruffly.

I've come this far and I'm not turning back now. I need to convince him somehow. We stay in silence for longer than is comfortable.

"Look, son," says Charon, breaking the silence. "The only way to cross the river is for me to row you. And my passengers have to be dead, and you're living."

"I'm not leaving until you let me cross," I say. I sit down on the riverbank and begin to play my lyre to pass the time.

I don't know why I didn't think of it earlier. Within minutes, I see Charon's eyes soften. His grimace relaxes into the smallest of smiles.

"I haven't heard music for years," he says wistfully.

I stop playing and look at him.

"Keep going, your song is majestic," he says.

"If you let me cross the river, I'll play for you." I pluck each string one by one. The notes chime and hang in the air.

"Climb aboard," he says. "Your song can be your payment."

"Gladly," I say, and begin to play.

I sing a song about the lost souls of the riverbank,

and how my heart is broken. It's a sad song and Charon is moved to tears. My heart feels lighter as I play. The thought of reaching the other side is daunting, but with each push of Charon's pole, I'm one step closer to Eurydice. When we reach the other side, the boat shudders to a standstill and I clamber onto the riverbank.

"I'll never forget your song," says Charon. "Now, you'll have to get past the gates of the Underworld next. I would wish you luck, but unfortunately, I don't think that will help. As soon as you meet Cerberus, I'm certain you'll come back and beg me to take you home."

11 The hound of Hades

On this side of the river, there's a stench in the air. Is this what the Underworld smells like? A fog hangs all around me, and shadows stretch across the stone floor. It feels like I'm deep underground. I look up but can't see a ceiling or anything but darkness. Flames flicker to the sides of me, from torches hung on the walls.

I don't know which way to go or what to do next. I know I need to pass the high gates to the Underworld but where and how? The ground rumbles beneath my feet like an earthquake. I stumble backwards. It rumbles again. What is that noise?

I edge slowly forwards, fearing what I'm about to encounter. My heart is racing and my breathing is raspy. My chest is tight, and I can't catch my next breath. The ground rumbles again. I close my eyes and try to slow my breathing down. I've got this far; I know I can keep going.

The rumbling is becoming ever louder. Should I turn around? But then, what could wait for me in that direction? Despite my fear, I keep on. There's a mound up ahead; perhaps that's the gates? As I draw closer, I see that it's a huge rock. The smell is pungent now, and I feel queasy. I lean against the rock, to take a moment's break. Suddenly, I feel a gust of wind upon my face. As I look ahead, I see that it's not wind. It's breath …

In front of me, is the most terrifying beast I've ever seen. Larger than any beast on Earth. It's huge and lying within a cave, blocking it from end to end. I realise the rumbling is coming from the creature. It's snoring. The smell is from the beast's breath. I need to pass this beast. Beyond it, I can see the massive gates to the Underworld. This must be Cerberus that Charon warned me about.

I'm sure I can sneak past without waking

it. As I grow closer, I can see that it's a giant guard dog. I creep past its head and gasp in shock. Cerberus hasn't one head, but three! There's drool dripping from one of its vast jaws onto half gnawed bones. As I try not to make a sound, I see the hound's tail thrash suddenly. I shriek. The dog has a snake for a tail!

Suddenly, Cerberus stirs. It raises one head and sniffs the air. The middle head follows suit. I think it's smelt me. Its ears prick up. I can tell it's listening. I take another step towards the gates. I'm only a few steps away, but to get there, I need to squeeze past the beast's tail.

Cerberus hears me.

It whips one of its heads round and snarls. Its fangs are as sharp as a sword. I race back to the huge rock, and only just make it! I crouch behind it. I can hear the hound snapping its jaws. I peer over the top. Cerberus is sniffing the ground, its eyes flash red with fire. It growls in my direction. Only the dead can pass through the gates to the Underworld. Cerberus is here to make sure of that. I realise that now.

There must be another route to the Underworld. I can see that there's no way I can pass the three-headed beast. As I'm about to head back the way I came, Cerberus roars. I stagger backwards, dropping my lyre. It clangs to the floor. Cerberus has heard, and begins heading in my direction, barking furiously. I grab my lyre.

My lyre!

I don't have any time to think it through. I can't outrun this beast, but maybe I can tame it. I tamed the wild beasts back home. Maybe my music will work on Cerberus too.

I strum the lyre with shaking hands, and hum along nervously. The hound howls mournfully, and then whimpers. I step out from behind the rock and pluck the strings one by one. I begin to sing, and Cerberus stretches and comes towards me. Its mouths gape open. I don't know what to do, so I carry on as I am. One of the heads draws towards me. Its breath is hot and overpowering. I don't know what will happen next …

It licks me, wags its snake-tail and sits by my side. I didn't expect that!

As I carry on playing, Cerberus calms and eventually lies down and falls back asleep. I stroke Cerberus's bronze fur coat gently, as I watch its body rise and fall with each breath. I return to strumming as I pass it. With all my might, I push the gigantic gates. They creak open and I squeeze through the gap and enter the Underworld. I'm so close to Eurydice now, I can almost sense her. I wonder if she can sense me. Now all I have to do is find Hades.

12 Into the Underworld

Cerberus is snoring in the distance. I creep onwards, further into the depths of the Underworld. I feel more determined than ever. I've managed to get this far; I'm certain I'll be able to find Hades and convince him.

It's lighter in the Underworld than I imagined. It feels like dusk – that time of day when it's not quite night-time yet, but the sunlight has faded. There's a chilly breeze rustling through the air, and I wrap my woollen shawl around me.

Ghosts shuffle beside me, going this way and that. I try not to make eye contact with them. I feel like a lost soul from the other side of the riverbank. I'm wandering aimlessly amongst these ghosts, not knowing which way to go. It all looks the same to me.

I play a sad melody on my lyre, echoing my feelings of loneliness inside. My song echoes throughout the Underworld, bouncing off the caverns and tunnels all around. I pass by someone rolling a gigantic rock up a hill. It takes me a few moments to realise who it is. I've heard tales of him – Sisyphus, the wicked king.

"Stop your staring," he growls.

I quickly look away and continue playing. I can't help but watch as he rolls a heavy, giant rock over and over up the hill. As soon as it's about to reach the top, it tumbles down again. He catches me looking at him again. I'm about to say sorry, but he speaks first.

"That music is beautiful." He wipes a tear from his eye and stops rolling his rock. King Sisyphus climbs upon it and tilts his head as he listens. "My punishment is to roll this rock forever, but your playing has compelled me to stop for a rest."

I nod to him and carry on my search for Hades. A little later, I turn to see he's rolling his rock once again, now I've passed.

I realise that I'm walking through the Asphodel Fields. The fields stretch on forever, as far as my eyes can see. The land is scattered with ghostly, grey flowers. This is a place where you forget all of your memories, but it doesn't work on me. I'm not dead, after all. Suddenly, my heart feels heavy. Does this mean Eurydice has forgotten me? Would this whole journey be worthless?

Here and there, ghosts pause in what they're doing to hear my melody. My music must be working its powers on them too, as a trail of ghosts begin to follow behind me.

A fog forms around me, and I can no longer see clearly. These fields seem never-ending, and I don't know whether to carry on forwards, or turn to the left or right. Which way should I go? I stop to gather my thoughts. I turn a little, wondering whether to go here or there. Suddenly, I've lost all my bearings, and I no longer know which way I'm facing. My songs become mixed up. I can't seem to find the right notes. I try to sing the songs I know, but the words evade me.

My heart is hammering, and my thoughts

are racing. I keep on walking, not knowing if I'm heading back towards the gates and Cerberus. What if I'm stuck here forever? I keep pressing forwards. Onwards and onwards. Finally, the fog seems to lift, and I see a road ahead of me.

I follow the road as it twists and turns until at last, I come upon a fork in the path. The ghosts leave me here, and I continue the next part of my journey alone. I take a deep breath. It's nearly time for me to confront Hades, but first there's a new challenge for me to face.

13 The three judges

I know instantly where I am. Three towering figures are opposite me, at the fork in the road. I'm faced with the three judges. I halt my playing and swallow nervously.

"Who comes before us?" speaks the tallest of the three. He swishes his cloak and bends over me. "I am Minos and I shall hear your case. Tell me why you think you are worthy of going to Elysium."

"I … um – " I stutter.

"Come now," speaks the middle one, in a deep voice. "State your case and I shall listen closely."

"Rhadamanthus, that's what I said just now," says Minos.

Rhadamanthus clears his throat. "And I was repeating it, Minos, to ensure this soul knew what to do!"

The third steps forward. "Once you have stated your case, we will confer and decide together! We're Minos, Rhadamanthus and Aeacus. Once we were mortals and, now, we are judges. We carry the great honour to judge all souls, so speak up! Speak up! State your case!"

The three of them look at me expectantly.

"Well … I – " I say. "I'm actually not – "

"He's not dead!" Minos shouts out. "He's not dead! We can't judge this soul because he is a mortal."

"Are you sure?"

They all step a little closer and peer at me.

I nod and sheepishly say, "It's true."

"You are lost!" declares Rhadamanthus.

"I am … can you direct me to Hades, please?"

As if he doesn't hear me, he repeats what he just said. "You are lost! Go back to where you came from. You do not belong here."

I sigh. This is getting me nowhere, so I try to walk past them. I need to get to Hades! My patience is evaporating by the second.

"Oh no, no, no!" says Aeacus. "You can't pass. You aren't dead."

"Let me explain," I say, and I begin to play my lyre. I sing them a song about my journey so far and how my loved one was taken too soon. As I stop playing, the three judges pat me on my back. They sniffle back tears and nod.

“Go on,” says Minos, in a whisper. “Go and win her back!”

The other two nod, and Minos points into the distance. “Head towards that mist, and you will find Hades.”

Before I leave, I have to ask, “Did you judge Eurydice? Where did she go?”

“Eurydice was kind of heart and good by nature,” says Aeacus. “She went to Elysium, you will be thankful to know.”

“Thank you,” I say. I’m pleased Eurydice was sent to a place reserved for people honoured by the gods, but that isn’t the place for her. Her place is by my side, and I’ll stop at nothing until I make that happen.

I hurry past the judges and keep going in the direction they showed me. My footsteps echo all around, and I continue my playing.

In the distance, I see a palace looming out of the mist. That must be where Hades is, and where I must go!

14 The palace of Hades

The palace seems out of place in this grey land. It's ink black with golden flecks. It feels daunting walking through the gigantic archway.

I carry on singing as I wander the labyrinth of halls, hoping I stumble upon the right place to find Hades.

However, somebody finds me first. It's Persephone – Hades' wife and queen of the Underworld.

"I thought I heard singing." Her voice is as sweet as honey. "And I did. Your playing is enchanting." Her demeanour is calming to me. She flicks her long flowing hair behind her ears and smiles at me. Her eyes suddenly light up. "My husband should hear you play!"

"That's why I'm here," I say.

I expect her to ask me why, but she doesn't.

Persephone turns, and gestures for me to follow. "This way," she says.

I carry on playing as I follow her, and I think about Persephone's own story. She only lives in the Underworld for six months of the year, and then she returns to her mother, Demeter, the goddess of harvest. Whenever she returns, her mother celebrates, causing plants to grow and blossom. When it's time for Persephone to return to her husband Hades, her mother's sadness causes the plants to shrivel and die until it's time for Persephone's return and once again, they regrow. The fact that Persephone can go between the Underworld and the land of the living shows me that it must be possible. If Persephone can go there, so can Eurydice! I clench my fists and fight back any negative thoughts. I need to think I can do this, to convince Hades.

We finally enter a grand room. The ceiling is as high as the sky. The room is airy and bright, unlike anywhere else in the Underworld. Light from flames glints off the golden walls and at the back I see two thrones, and Hades is sitting on one. My time has come. This is the moment I've been waiting for. I know what I have to do.

"What's all this, Persephone?" asks Hades, from high up on his golden throne. His pitchfork and helmet are lying at his feet.

I'd always imagined Hades to be this terrifying, ghastly god, but he looks just like a man. He wears a grave expression, as though he's carrying the weight of the world on his shoulders.

“I heard this wonderful song floating through the palace halls. I followed the sound, and it was this lyre player here!” says Persephone, smiling sweetly. “You have to hear his song! I know you’ll love it.”

"There's no time for such frivolities! I have to keep focused on my job," says Hades. "And why, may I ask, is this lyre player that you mention even here? He's clearly not supposed to be in the Underworld. This man is alive!" He grabs his pitchfork and bangs it twice on the floor. The ground under my feet vibrates.

I step cautiously towards him, ready to state my case and play for him. "My name is Orpheus, and I have a request – " I begin.

"How dare you approach me!" bellows Hades, cutting me off. "Step back at once!"

I shrink backwards. Maybe I was right to feel fearful of Hades! I've never felt so small. I've never felt so out of place. Here I stand, in my ragged clothes, dishevelled from my long journey, in the most breathtaking room I've ever seen. Everything in this room is golden. It's so bright that I have to squint.

Hades turns to Persephone. "I know you adore music, my love. I thank you for thinking of me, but this man has no place here. And I have no time to even consider listening to some music. There's so much work to be done. I have to ensure the dead stay in the Underworld and don't escape!"

"Hades, his is a song worth listening to. I've never felt so moved by music before. I felt as if flowers were blooming in my heart."

Hades looks at her, and I can see his eyes softening. He reaches out to her and takes her hand. They stare at each other longingly, and my heart aches. I remember that feeling so well and it was snatched from me.

"For me, Hades. Please let us listen to him together," Persephone says gently.

"Very well," he says, stroking his long beard. "For you. Only for you."

Persephone takes her place on the throne next to his. Hades nods at me, and I step forward again.

"I have a request, Hades," I say.

"What is it you want?" His voice changes tone when he speaks to me. It's no longer the soft voice he used when he spoke to Persephone. He sounds impatient.

"My dear wife was taken from me too soon. We never got to spend even one day together as a married couple. Please can you return her to me? You're the only one who can."

"Why should I return her?" he asks, narrowing his eyes at me. "What's so special about this wife of yours, above other wives? Why, if every husband or wife came to me and asked for their loved ones to return, the Underworld would be empty!"

I know that there's only one way I can make him understand. I lift my lyre and begin to play a ballad for them both. I sing about the first day I met Eurydice. I sing about how she brought sunshine into my life. Then, my song slows down and I sing about the day Eurydice was taken from me.

Persephone and Hades are visibly moved by my song. They both dab their eyes and hold each other's hands tightly.

When I finish, Hades clears his throat. "Orpheus, for half the year Persephone goes up to the land of the living, and it's torturous for me. I always miss her so much. I can't imagine myself in your position, and never seeing her ever again." He looks to Persephone. "Go and get the three sisters. We need them to bring Eurydice back to life."

I gasp. My voice is caught in my throat. I try to speak, but no words come. I try again. "Thank you," I whisper hoarsely.

"There's one condition though!" says Hades. "You need to show me you're taking this seriously. It's unheard of for the dead to return to the living. You must follow my instructions and not break this condition."

"Anything! Anything!" I cry.

"Once Eurydice is brought back to life, you can escort her back up to the sunlight. However, you mustn't look back until the sun is shining upon you."

I nod eagerly.

"As long as you don't look back," he reminds me. "Eurydice will return."

My heart is leaping at the thought of Eurydice being by my side again.

15 A promise made

I hear the sisters mumbling before I see them. All three are as wrinkled as each other. They're as old as time itself and they have an important role in the world. One spins the thread of life, one measures the length of the thread, and the third cuts it when a person's life is over. They make their way towards Hades, and each bow to him in turn.

"Clotho, Lachesis and Atropos, I've called you here before me, as I have an unusual request." His voice booms throughout the palace.

Their eyes are wide with wonder as they listen to Hades.

"A little while ago, you cut the thread of

somebody. I would like you to mend that thread and bring her back to life," says Hades.

Clotho gasps. "That's unheard of!"

"But possible," says Lachesis, rubbing her chin thoughtfully.

"Who is this person?" asks Atropos.

"Eurydice," says Hades.

"I can do it," says Atropos. "I will mend her thread of life."

"Thank you," Hades says.

"It'll take a few minutes," she says. "But not long."

It takes even less time than she says, and suddenly, I see my dear Eurydice appear beside Hades' throne. She's as beautiful today as the first day we met. Her eyes twinkle in the darkness, and when they meet mine, they brighten even more.

"The time has come," says Hades. "Go. Lead her

back. Remember the condition! Remember, it's forbidden to look back at her until you're both out of the Underworld."

"I won't forget," I say. I look to him and then the sisters. "Thank you! Thank you!"

"It's rare for the living to enter the Underworld, Orpheus, and it's unheard of for the living to enter a second time," says Hades. "The next time you come here, it'll be because you are no longer mortal, and are here for eternity."

"Can you remember the way back?" says Persephone.

I nod.

I don't wait another second, and turn back the way I came, with Eurydice behind me! We make our way back through the halls of the palace. I remind myself to keep going and not turn to look back. Just a little further, and then we'll be back with the living!

Relief floods throughout every vein in my body. The risky journey is over and I've succeeded!

I almost can't believe it.

I play my lyre as we go. The rhythm skips along with my footsteps. As we pass the three judges, they cheer me on.

"Keep going, Orpheus!"

"You did it!"

They don't seem intimidating at all now. They no longer seem like three towering judges, just three wise, old, bearded men.

The Asphodel Fields lie ahead of me. They don't seem as grey as before. The flowers look beautiful, in fact. The fields seem to stretch to infinity. I can't wait to get to the other side, and then it's just Cerberus and Charon to get past! I quicken my pace.

Finally, the fields make way for the stony path, and I can see the gates ahead of me, far off in the distance. Cerberus's snores reverberate through the air. I creep forwards and past the gates. I ensure I keep playing to keep Cerberus sleeping. Nearly there! I take a deep breath and sneak past the snoozing hound. I can see the river ahead of me.

"Charon!" I call. "Can you take us on your boat for one last time until we meet again, when our time has finally come to join the Underworld."

Charon nods. "I'll gladly take you both across, if you'll play for me again." He chuckles to himself. "I didn't think you'd do it, Orpheus, but you've surpassed my expectations!"

As I climb aboard, I feel the boat sway.

It must be Eurydice climbing in after me. I stay looking straight ahead though! I play for the whole journey across the dark river. A dense fog hangs in the air.

When we reach the other side, I clamber out and keep going. The cavern is ahead of us now. Finally, I can see a hint of light. The sunlight is beaming through at the far end. I'm so close to having Eurydice back with me!

16 Keeping your word

The way up the cavern is steep and hard going. I'm so close to seeing Eurydice again. I long to see her beauty once more. I long to hear her sweet voice and feel her hand in mine. Suddenly, I realise I haven't heard Eurydice since we left the boat. I stop playing and listen closely. I can't hear her steps. I can't hear her breaths.

"Eurydice?" I call.

There's no reply.

Is she still behind me? My heart trembles at the thought that she isn't. I don't have a choice though. I need to keep going. I'll know for certain when we reach the sunlight. Surely, she must still be there?

Doubt seeps into my mind. I feel the need to check. How would Hades know if I had? Surely one little glimpse wouldn't hurt?

A panicked thought occurs to me. What if it's all been a dreadful trick by Hades? What if I reach the sunlight and she's not there? I couldn't bear that to happen.

Step by step, the thought strengthens. I'm sure of it now. This was a trick. Eurydice isn't behind me. Maybe I imagined the boat swaying and Hades has lied to me. What a fool I've been! Who would trust a god of the Underworld? Why would he return Eurydice to me?

Hades even said it himself. If he returned every loved one to their husbands and wives, the Underworld would be empty … so, of course, he wouldn't do it for me.

She's not there. I can feel it in my bones. I need to turn around and go back and get her. I need to make sure she really is there. A cold wind gusts through the air and I shiver.

A few more steps and I'll be in the sunlight, and

it'll be too late to turn around. They wouldn't let me through the Underworld again, of that, I'm sure!

I'm about to take a step into the sunlight. I can't risk going without her. Hades has certainly deceived me, I decide. I turn my head to look.

Eurydice is there! Just as Hades promised. But then she stretches her hand to me.

"Eurydice!" I cry.

Her auburn hair flows into the shadows like a river and she gradually fades from view.

I reach my arms out into nothingness. "EURYDICE!"

How could I have been so reckless and turned around?

Just then, Hades suddenly appears. He's holding his helmet, which had the power to make him invisible.

"I've been following the whole way," says Hades.

Of course he has!

I feel like an empty shell.

"Has she … has she – " I can't say the words.

"She's gone back to the Underworld," says Hades. "Like I said she would. You had one condition, and you broke your promise!"

"But I … I – " I stutter, falling to my knees at his feet. "I needed to check. To know she was really there … to know that – ”

“That I’d keep my word?” roars Hades. “But you couldn’t keep yours!”

I clasp my hands together and beg Hades. “Please return her to me. Please. I’m begging you!”

Hades shakes his head. “You had one condition, and you didn’t meet it. I never go back on my word.” Before fading from view, he whispers, “You will be with Eurydice again one day, Orpheus, but not until it’s your time to join the Underworld. Go back to the sunlight and enjoy the rest of your life.”

And with that, he disappears from view, leaving me alone in the dark cavern. I sit in the opening, and I play a mournful song on my lyre. No person should have to be parted from their loved one twice! My heart aches with guilt for turning around. I don’t know what to do next.

I stay sitting there as I watch the sunlight disappear through the opening ahead of me. I think and think about what I should do. I decide to try to go back and convince Hades again.

I climb down the steep path and make my way back to the water's edge.

"Please, Charon," I beg. "Let me board your boat!"

"I have my orders," Charon says. "And I'm not allowed."

It is as Hades said: no living person can enter the Underworld twice. I strum a mournful song on my lyre, but Charon looks the other way. I play ten more songs, but he doesn't stir. I can't convince him this time.

Sadly, I turn and clamber back up the steep path, my legs heavy with heartache. I take a first step back into the sunlight.

Father is there, waiting for me. "Oh, Orpheus, my son," he says. "I see Eurydice is not with you."

I don't need to explain, he can see how distraught I am.

"I'm a fool!" I sob into his chest. "All I had to do was trust in Hades." I explain what happened and Hades' one condition.

"Nobody could blame you for having doubts, my son," says Father. "One day, you'll be reunited with Eurydice, and when you are, your lyre will become a constellation of stars in the sky. When anyone looks upon them, they'll remember you and how strong your love for Eurydice was."

I know in my heart that he's right and remember Hades' last words to me. *"You will be with Eurydice again one day."*

Our mortal love was cut too short but, one day, we'll be reunited. I pick up my lyre, and I make a promise to myself that I'll sing my story as I travel to places far and wide and play for anyone who will listen. I will keep Eurydice's memory alive through my song for the rest of my days.

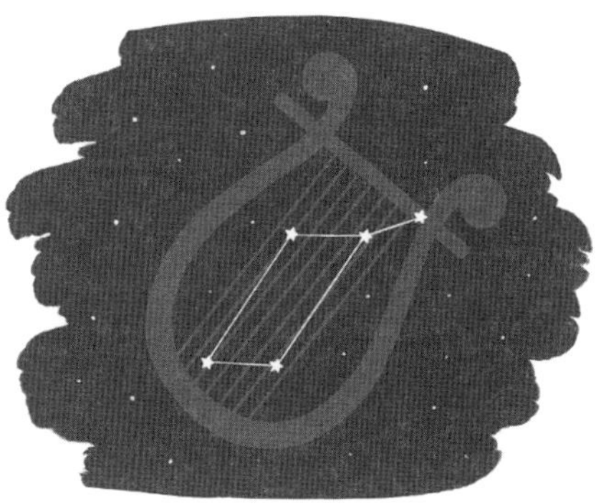

Book talk questions

How does Orpheus's music impact the people and gods around him?

What does Orpheus's journey to the Underworld reveal about his character?

Why does Hades agree to bring Eurydice back, and what does he hope to teach Orpheus in return?

Why do you think Orpheus turned back to look at Eurydice?

How does the myth reflect themes of love, grief, and the power of music?

How does Orpheus's relationship with Eurydice change throughout the story?

How does Orpheus's decision at the end of the story change the fate of both himself and Eurydice?

What lessons does Orpheus learn about trust and the consequences of doubt?

What role does fate play in Orpheus and Eurydice's story?

Have you read any other myths or legends?

Ask the author

How did you start writing, and what do you enjoy about it?

As a child, I loved writing stories and poems, but it wasn't until I became a mum that I decided I'd like to be an author.

I love all aspects of writing – from the initial nugget of an idea, to editing a story until it feels "just right".

What inspired you to write a modern retelling of this Greek myth?

As a teenager, I studied the Latin poem "Orpheus and Eurydice". The story has stuck with me ever since.

Do you have a favourite place to write?

I love writing at my desk (which is cluttered with my favourite books and lots of notebooks).

Which book world would you like to live in?

I'd like to live in a magical world. I'd be so inspired by the magic, that I'd write a story about it!

Why do you think the myth of Orpheus and Eurydice has resonated with so many cultures?
The myth covers the universal themes of love, loss, temptation, determination and the power of music, that everyone can relate to.

What challenges did you face in bringing this myth to life for a younger audience?
I wanted to be sensitive to the difficult themes in the myth and didn't want to gloss over Orpheus's feelings. Another challenge was writing a setting that reflected life for ancient Greeks.

How does music influence the story?
Orpheus's music is a driving force for the story. Without it, Orpheus couldn't have made his way through the Underworld.

What do you hope readers will take away from Orpheus's journey to the Underworld?
I hope readers will appreciate Orpheus's determination. Pursuing a goal is hard when we face obstacles, but by persevering, we can often overcome them. Orpheus *did* meet his goal of confronting Hades, but unfortunately temptation was too much for him.

Collins
BIG CAT

Published by Collins
An imprint of HarperCollins*Publishers*

The News Building
1 London Bridge Street
London SE1 9GF
UK

Macken House
39/40 Mayor Street Upper
Dublin 1
D01 C9W8
Ireland

10 9 8 7 6 5 4 3 2 1

ISBN 978-0-00-874492-2

British Library Cataloguing-in-Publication Data
A catalogue record for this publication is available from the British Library.

Author: Emily Ann Davison
Illustrator: Sunnu Rebecca Choi
Publisher: Laura White
Commissioning editor: Holly Woolnough
Development editor: Zoë Clarke
Product manager: Holly Woolnough
Content editor: Selin Akca
Copyeditor: Sally Byford
Proofreader: Catherine Dakin
Reviewer: Lisa Davis
Cover designer: Sarah Finan
Internal design: 2Hoots Publishing Services Ltd
Typesetter: Jouve India Ltd
Production controller: Katharine Willard

Collins would like to thank the teachers and children at Grange Primary School, Southwark, for being part of the development of Big Cat Read On.

Printed in the UK.

FSC
www.fsc.org
MIX
Paper | Supporting responsible forestry
FSC™ C007454

This book contains FSC™ certified paper and other controlled sources to ensure responsible forest management.

For more information visit: www.harpercollins.co.uk/green

Made with responsibly sourced paper and vegetable ink

Scan to see how we are reducing our environmental impact.